This book belongs to.

_____

This book is dedicated to
my boys whose lives inspire
and bless me everyday

Marvin Mouse Meets the Baby King

By Michelle L Hoy

There once was a mouse named Marvin
Yes, Marvin Mouse was his name
He lived in a hole
In a tiny horse stall
In a barn in Bethlehem

Nothing much usually happened
In that barn from day to day
But that changed in an instant
When a man and his missus
Came one night in the barn to stay

He sat in the corner and watched
In amazement at what his eyes saw
From the woman was born
A sweet baby boy
Wrapped in rags then placed in a trough

How exciting this was for young Marvin
A new baby, he'd never seen
So out from the corner
He moved in a bit closer
For a better look at things

Suddenly from outside the barn
Came some shepherds proclaiming with glee
An angel appeared
And told us that here
Lies the child that shall be our king

A king? Marvin wondered
A king! Well how could that be
Then he looked one more time
At the face of the child
And knew that his Savior he'd seen

Marvin decided from that day forward
A follower he'd always be
To walk beside this young baby boy
Who would be known for all time
As King

THE END

Things to think about...

Who was the baby?

Why do you think Marvin decided to follow the baby who would be King?

What does the word Savior mean?

Luke 2

King James Version

And it came to pass in those days, that there went out a decree from Caesar Augustus that all the world should be taxed.

2. (And this taxing was first made when Cyrenius was governor of Syria.)

3. And all went to be taxed, every one into his own city.

4. And Joseph also went up from Galilee, out of the city of Nazareth, into Judaea, unto the city of David, which is called Bethlehem; (because he was of the house and lineage of David:)

5. To be taxed with Mary his espoused wife, being great with child.

6. And so it was, that, while they were there, the days were accomplished that she should be delivered.

7. And she brought forth her firstborn son, and wrapped him in swaddling clothes, and laid him in a manger; because there was no room for them in the inn.

8. And there were in the same country shepherds abiding in the field, keeping watch over their flock by night.

9. And, lo, the angel of the Lord came upon them, and the glory of the Lord shone round about them: and they were sore afraid.

10. And the angel said unto them, Fear not: for, behold, I bring you good tidings of great joy, which shall be to all people.

11. For unto you is born this day in the city of David a Saviour, which is Christ the Lord.

12. And this shall be a sign unto you; Ye shall find the babe wrapped in swaddling clothes, lying in a manger.

13. And suddenly there was with the angel a multitude of the heavenly host praising God, and saying,

14. Glory to God in the highest, and on earth peace, good will toward men.

15. And it came to pass, as the angels were gone away from them into heaven, the shepherds said one to another, Let us now go even unto Bethlehem, and see this thing which is come to pass, which the Lord hath made known unto us.

16. And they came with haste, and found Mary, and Joseph, and the babe lying in a manger.

17. And when they had seen it, they made known abroad the saying which was told them concerning this child.

18. And all they that heard it wondered at those things which were told them by the shepherds.

19. But Mary kept all these things, and pondered them in her heart.

About the Author:

Michelle Hoy was born, raised, and still remains in Iowa where she and her husband have raised their two sons, and share their home with their two very spoiled and loved puppin "babies" Jasper and Diggory.

Michelle has ministered as a praise and worship leader for over 15 years, has written, performed, and recorded her own music, some of which has been featured on radio programs and short films, and contributes articles to a faith based web community.

Marvin Mouse Meets the Baby King is Michelle's first children's book.

Stay up to date with Michelle L Hoy
and upcoming projects at
www.MichelleLHoy.com

Follow Michelle on Facebook @MarvinMouseBooks

Written by Michelle L. Hoy
Illustrated by Jasmine Bailey
Graphic design and formatting by Misty Black Media, LLC

Library of Congress Control Number: 2020923656
ISBN Paperback 978-1-7362855-0-3

First Edition 2020

www.MichelleLHoy.com

Made in the USA
Coppell, TX
26 December 2020